MW01119666

HOLLY
THE DEAF DALMATIAN

"HOLLY GETS A NEW HOME"

LISA MARTIN

DRAWINGS BY
SHANNON DARCH

Order this book online at www.trafford.com
or email orders@trafford.com

Most Trafford titles are also available at major online book retailers.

Illustrations by Shannon Darch

Permission granted by Dalmatian Adoption & Rescue for the use of their website address.

Edited by Carol Ovenden

Printed in the United States of America.

ISBN: 978-1-4269-4531-1

Library of Congress Control Number: 2010915294

Our mission is to efficiently provide the world's finest, most comprehensive book publishing service, enabling every author to experience success. To find out how to publish your book, your way, and have it available worldwide, visit us online at www.trafford.com

Trafford rev. 10/26/2010

 www.trafford.com

North America & international
toll-free: 1 888 232 4444 (USA & Canada)
phone: 250 383 6864 ♦ fax: 812 355 4082

for DAR

HOLLY

Lisa Martin

Holly was a cute little puppy covered in spots...
Holly is a Dalmatian.

Holly was not a happy puppy, though, because she didn't have a family to love.

You see, Holly is a special girl...she is deaf. That means she can't
hear anyone talking to her or hear birds chirping or cats meowing,

but Holly can understand body language. She knows if you are happy by your smile...

...or mad by your frown.

Holly lived with the Dalmatian Rescue people who look after Dalmatians that need a home.

One day, they took Holly to a pet show and set up a booth to show Holly off to everyone. Holly had so much fun meeting people, especially children.

Then a lady named Lisa came to see Holly and instantly fell in love with her.

Lisa already had a Dalmatian that could hear. Lisa also knew how to train dogs and wanted Holly to come and live with her.

So Holly went to visit Lisa and her family.

When Holly met Jazz, the hearing Dalmatian, they played and played and played!

Holly was so happy! That night she went to sleep in her brand new bed with a big smile on her face and dreamed of running and playing!

Holly had a new home and a family to love!